Children's Books:
Who Took My Banana?

Sally Huss

Nothing is better than a banana for breakfast,

Better than strawberries and cream.

I would love a banana for breakfast. This is my wish.

This is my dream.

An orangutan awoke one morning, reached under her pillow of leaves, looking for the banana she planned on for breakfast. But, it wasn't there.

"Who took my banana?" she yelled. No one answered.

So off she went into the rainforest to find out who took her banana.

She came upon a green mamba snake who had a big lump in his belly.

"Did you take my banana?" the orangutan asked.

"Me? No! I never eat bananas. I like a good mouse though."

"Humph!" the orangutan grunted. Off she went looking for her banana and getting hungrier by the minute.

Banana, banana, there is nothing like a banana.

I could eat one on cereal. I could eat one on toast,

But I like to eat a banana plain the most.

A sloth hung on a branch among the forest trees. "Did you take my banana?" called the orangutan.

"I hardly know what one looks like," said the sloth. "I prefer to eat leaves, buds, and tender roots. If you have any of those, I'd be happy to take them off your hands."

"Not likely," said the orangutan, noticing that she was becoming ruder and ruder the hungrier and hungrier she got. "Sorry," she said, as she swung down to the forest floor.

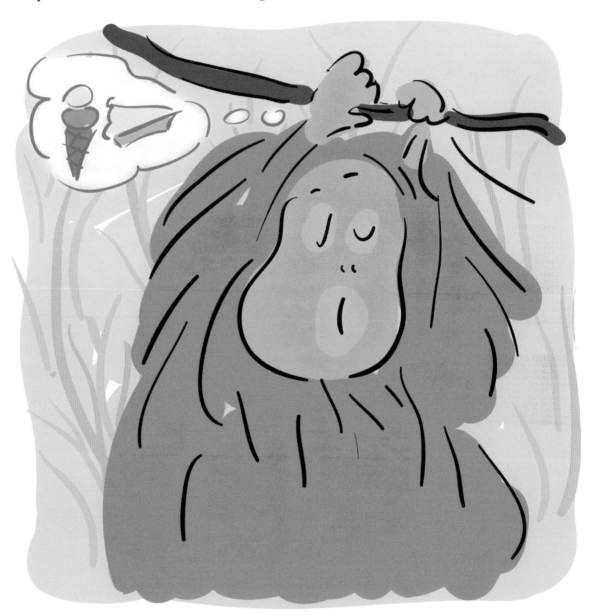

Bananas are delicious in ice cream and pie.
If I don't find my banana soon, I think I shall die.

She came upon a tapir and asked, "Did you take my banana?"

"No," said the tapir. "I do love a banana now and then, but I've just had my fill of berries and I couldn't eat another thing. Good luck in finding your banana though."

"Thanks," said the orangutan, moving along a lane on the forest floor.

A banana and peanut butter sandwich is tasty and good,

But right now I could eat a banana any way that I could.

An elephant was on her way to a watering hole.

"Did you take my banana?" she shouted out to the elephant.

"Are you kidding? What would I do with one little banana? I'd need a truckload full. I am very fond of bananas, but I'd need more than even a bunch."

"Sorry," said the orangutan, feeling that she had insulted the elephant.

Still hungry and hoping to find her banana, she moved on to the watering hole.

A banana shake is delicious. Banana bread is nutritious.

But a plain, simple banana right now would satisfy my wishes.

At the watering hole she waved to a crocodile.

"Did you take my banana?" she asked rather timidly. She knew better than to anger a crocodile.

"I have no use for a banana," said the croc, but if you come a little closer I could tell you what I do like to eat."

"No. That's fine. I'm only interested in finding my banana."

She also knew better than to get too close to the croc.

I've eaten a banana salad and even banana soup

And when I've had banana ice cream, I've needed an extra scoop.

Across the pond, the orangutan spotted a spotted leopard.

"Yoo-hoo," she yelled. "Did you take my banana?"

"Are you asking ME if I took your banana? Why would I do that? I like to eat those things that eat bananas. Do you eat bananas?" the leopard inquired.

"Well, not at the moment," replied the orangutan, now hungrier than she could ever remember.

Bananas make a great snack in the middle of the day,

But morning is my favorite time to eat one, I really must say.

Heading back into the rainforest, the orangutan noticed a
chameleon sitting on a twig. "Did you take my banana?" she asked
the shy, but colorful chameleon.

"My, my, no. I would be afraid it would change my color to yellow and then I wouldn't be able to hide in the leaves. Good luck on finding it though."

"Thanks," answered the orangutan who was now becoming quite depressed, as well as hungry.

Nothing is more delicious than a banana muffin

Filled with a raisin or two.

If I had a dozen, it would still be too few.

A band of monkeys was flying through the trees. The orangutan called up to them, "Did any of you take my banana?"

"I wish we had. We love bananas. But, no, we didn't. When you find it, will you share it with us?"

"No! I'm starved! I need to eat the whole thing myself, if I can just find it."

Bananas cookies and banana tea,

Anything made with bananas would please me.

"Squawk. Squawk," a toucan bellowed from a high perch.

"What's all the commotion?" he asked.

"I'm looking for my banana. Did you take my banana?"

"I wish I had. I love bananas, especially with ice cream. I love everything with ice cream – insects, berries, lizards, and bananas. No, I didn't take your banana."

A plain banana, a banana in punch,

A banana stew, dried bananas to crunch —

There is nothing as good to eat or to drink.

That's how delicious a banana is. That's what I think!

The orangutan had made a complete circle of the rainforest and now returned to her nest, tired and very, very hungry.

As she lay down on her nest to rest again, she heard the smacking of lips and smelled the sweet fragrance of banana floating through the air.

She sat up…

… then got up and looked at the branch above her where her baby had been sleeping in his own nest of leaves.

There he lay, snuggled up on his bed, munching on his mother's very own banana.

"Oh," sighed his proud mother. "Now I know who took my banana and I couldn't be happier."

Yes, a banana is something I truly love,

But it is even better when it is eaten by someone I love!

The end,
but not the end
of sharing with
those you love.

At the end of this book you will find a Certificate of Merit that may be issued to any child who promises to honor the requirements stated in the Certificate. This fine Certificate will easily fit into a 5"x7" frame, and happily suit any girl or boy who receives it!

Here is another fun, rhyming book by Sally Huss.

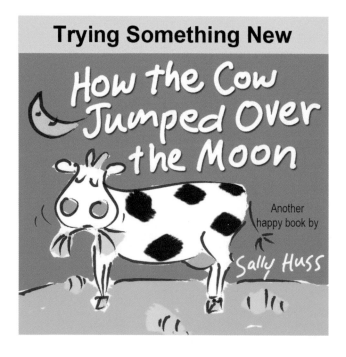

Description: A very stubborn, bored, and uninspired cow is steadfast in her determination not to try something new. She is amusingly invited to join one animal after the next in an adventure with them, but sticks to her old habits. It is not until a chicken encourages her to jump over the moon that she decides to change her ways.

All in rhyme, and all with a smile, this story is one to delight every child, and subtly spark the spirit of adventure within them. It emphasizes the importance of trying something new -- being adventurous and in the most whimsical way.

Charmingly illustrated in bright and happy colors.

To learn more about HOW THE COW JUMPED OVER THE MOON use this URL -- http://amzn.com/B004WOWQXY.

If you liked WHO TOOK MY BANANA? please be kind enough to post a short review on Amazon by using this URL: http://amzn.com/B00RHF20EK.

You may wish to join our Family of Friends to receive information about upcoming FREE e-book promotions and download a free poster – The Importance Happiness on Sally's website -- http://www.sallyhuss.com. Thank You.

More Sally Huss books may be viewed on the Author's Profile on Amazon. Here is that URL: http://amzn.to/VpR7B8.

About the Author/Illustrator

Sally Huss

   "Bright and happy," "light and whimsical" have been the catch phrases attached to the writings and art of Sally Huss for over 30 years. Sweet images dance across all of Sally's creations, whether in the form of children's books, paintings, wallpaper, ceramics, baby bibs, purses, clothing, or her King Features syndicated newspaper panel "Happy Musings."

   Sally creates children's books to uplift the lives of children and hopes you will join her in this effort by helping spread her happy messages.

   Sally is a graduate of USC with a degree in Fine Art and through the years has had 26 of her own licensed art galleries throughout the world.

This certificate may be cut out, framed, and presented to any child who has demonstrated her or his worthiness to receive it.

Certificate of Merit

_____
(Name)

The child named above is awarded this Certificate of Merit for honoring his or her parent(s), grandparents, teacher or coach by being:
*Respectful and attentive
*Helpful at home and in school
*Friendly to everyone

Presented by: _____   Date: _____

Printed in Great Britain
by Amazon.co.uk, Ltd.,
Marston Gate.